The Biggest Bear
in the Wood

Written by Joshua George
Illustrated by Megan Higgins

IMAGINE THAT

Licensed exclusively to Imagine That Publishing Ltd
Tide Mill Way, Woodbridge, Suffolk, IP12 1AP, UK
www.imaginethat.com
Copyright © 2021 Imagine That Group Ltd
All rights reserved
0 2 4 6 8 9 7 5 3 1
Manufactured in China

Written by Joshua George
Illustrated by Megan Higgins

ISBN 978-1-80105-196-5

A catalogue record for this book is available from the British Library

Look at me,

I'm feeling good,

I'm the biggest bear in the wood!

I've got big paws,   I've got big claws,

Look at me,

I'm feeling bad,

Those other bears made me feel sad!

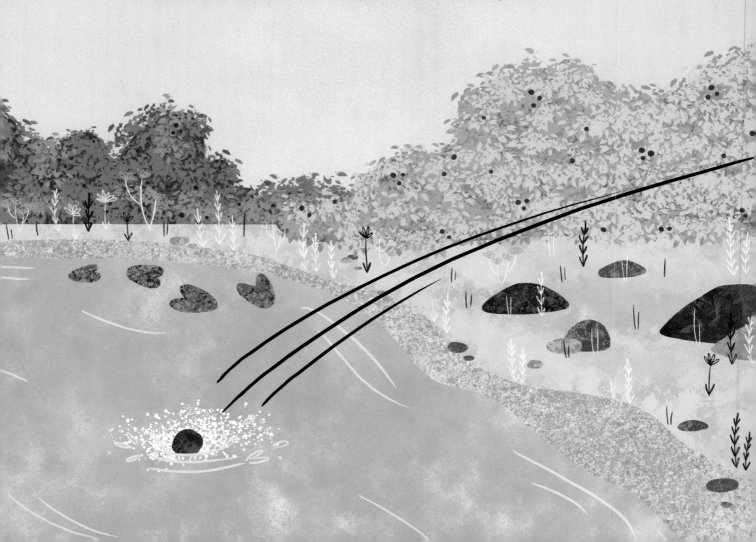

I've got small paws,

I've got small claws,

Look at me,

I'm in the wood,

I'm feeling good, like a bear should,

I'm not the biggest bear of all,

But then again,

I'm not that small!

And that's not how the story ends ...

Because now I've got some new bear friends!